I0610563

OUIJA BOARD

ME, THE OUIJA BOARD
AND MY ANCIENT "FRIEND".

JULIAN BLACK

First Edition: January 2019
Printed in the United States of America
ISBN: 1645500128
ISBN: 9781645500124

Dedication

For my favourite Horror film forever the Exorcist I watched this film when I was very young and it has Psychologically scarred me for life. This movie will never leave me simply because it questions is there such a thing as the Devil and hell in the after life and who gets to go there. Why is the after life such a complete mystery to Human Beings?.

A SHORT STORY OF DEMONIC POSSESSION

I was a lonley guy being lonley was a huge part of my life since I was young and well it has stayed with me I guess. Nothing much really happened in my life it was just a life of routine and I lived in a world that I felt invisible in and I guess I just excisted and fed and watered myself.

I worked in an office full of executives and people in suits and I was basically a gofer to them and slave if they said jump I jumped high if they wanted to put their feet up on me they could have my life was wonderful and every year got better and better but I was a survivior. They saw me as the office dumbo and that was how the building deemed me so there was no hope of making friends or having an office romance because if you get bracketed then it becomes universal to all and everybody.

I lived In a small shed of a place it was a place on it's own and Isolated my nearest neighbour was about half a mile away and my little place was tucked away behind trees and I had a little bit of land out back and out front with a fence around the back and a little wooden gate out the front with a garage and drive. Even In the summer months my house was dark because it was covered by trees, my house had the same bleakness to it that was also a huge part of my life.

I had social Isolation and I had some serious Issues with myself concerning my sexuality my sexuality was the main problem with me really and it just had a knock on effect with my life as a whole my job, my social circle, Intimacy, and getting on with life all things which give us humans a good and healthy quality of life.

I had no visitors to my house not even family members so once I got home it was just me and the house until the following day when I would get together with the office which I would not look forward to the majority of the time.

I could have gone out after work and found a pub or bar but I did not want to get close to anybody or make friends with anybody or let anybody into my life because I did not want acceptance to who I was and having friends and a social circle would mean communicating and letting people into my life and I did not want anybody to come into my life I mean maybe I did but I was afraid for this to happen. So I went on everyday as a routine but it was a very unhappy routine but it was one I was used too I really wanted a friend but it seemed impossible to find one or was I my own very worst enemy.

I was cleaning out my attic one day as my house was very small and I thought I could make the attic another space and make more room for myself really as nobody ever came to my house and I came across something which has always terrified me to death and a thing I have always looked at as dark and dangerous and evil it was a very old ouija board still in it's box and full of dust I picked it up and threw it to the floor as I did not even want to touch it or have any contact with the thing.

I just stared at it and I could not believe that something like this could be near me or in the same room as me a cold shiver of fear ran down my spine and body because I knew it was connected with evil and evil always frightened me as it does anybody after all fear is a human condition it is just some of us have more of it in our lives than others without making more connection with it.

I did not want to have anything to do with it and I was annoyed very annoyed that somebody or people had played with this in my house at some point and I wanted it gone from under my roof.

I did not want to touch it or feel it incase I cut myself on it or something happened like maybe it could attack me this is how scared I was of something like this and this was how my Imagination looked at a board like this. So I got my dust pan and brush and picked it up with this so that I would not have to touch it with my hands.

I picked it up with the dustpan and it fell out of the dustpan and through my attic door and down onto the landing of my house and I thought great I panicked and looked down through the hatch and on my carpet was the ouija board which had come out of it's box and the board now lying face down on my carpet I never wanted this to even be on my carpet and I should have left it where it was but I did not. I got the impression this board wanted to be noticed and it was making sure I noticed it it as if it was waiting to be found by the right person at the right time.

I feel evil prays on the vunerable wheather this be in the real world or in another world but it does like people who are already having problems which is why it is called evil I guess.

I went down through the attic door and stood over the ouija board and I did not know what to do as I hated the thing with a passion so I got my brush and brushed it back into the box and brushed the box into a bag and put it on my table ready for it to be thrown away and out of my house.

I sat in my chair and wondered if there really was a chance of me communicating with another world or with another person or another thing through a board that had been talked about since my parents days. I knew my mother had tried it in her youth and knew lots of other people who had many tales to say about the famous ouija board but it is up to the Individual if they wish or choose to believe the tales but I did believe and that is what scared me so much I did believe that contact with something or somebody through the board would be possible I just believed in these things.

I think if you want it hard enough and you want to believe in contact with another world or another dimension then it will happen I just feel vunerable people want it so much that it could happen. People with a pesimistic or arrogant attitude about such things and see it as a joke then to them it may not want to communicate because of their belief system but to people who it frightens and believe in such forces it really could work and communication could well be possible but evil lurks in the world today and in worlds past evil is very strong and the ouija board and evil go hand in hand it is very rare a board that people deem as good.

I could not help thinking that maybe if I had a go at it maybe if I just tried it maybe if I just looked at it I was transfixed by it and scared to death at the same time, my mind kept saying no throw it away put it out of this house but my body wanted to walk over to it pull it out of it's bag and it's box and lay it on my table and just stare at it and wonder what all the fuss is about and had I been watching far too many horror movies.

I left it on my table for days and did not touch it but I did not want to throw it out either because I was sure I would be able to communicate with another world and with other people but would this be a good thing to do and would I be able to handle it.

I wondered who I would want to communicate with if I was to talk with someone and who I would want to contact if the board was to ask me and it would have to be somebody from a time before God or Jesus christ or the roman catholic church and it would have to be a guy who liked men or who slept with men aswell as women and a time where sleeping with men was allowed and nobody thought anything of it so yes a time way before the roman catholic church ever existed or before judgement ever existed.

I thought maybe about contacting a young roman slave who was used by his owners for cleaning and cooking aswell as sexual commands which would have to have been obeyed or he would have been whipped and beaten for saying no a young guy who lived a life of pain and cruelty and lived to obey and please others and being totally afraid to have a mind of his own and even a voice of his own until In the end he lost who he really was and even what his life was all about or a male prostitute who got by by taking money off people for sexual needs.

It would have to be somebody who had experienced pain in their lives and a person who had never had life so easy but who could relate to me not because he was afraid of who he was but because he would come from a time where judgement was not known but because he was used for a life that was not his but a life living to please others.

I did not want to contact some ego centric arrogant well to do person who everybody obeyed and bowed down to just because he was well to do and had power and authority this was not what I needed there were and are enough of these in todays times without contacting somebody like this from long ago.

For days and weeks I thought about giving it a try and letting somebody see into our world today through my eyes and let them know how same sex people have a difficult time of it compared to their times maybe they could help me with my Issues but would it be good help or bad and was I willing to let fear keep me away from using the ouija board to make contact with a homosexual or bi - sexual person but from a different time. I was far too scared to make contact with a homosexual from our time but what about a homosexual from a time that goes way back to before the almighty and the devil itself. (or would satan want to have something to do with this and would I have a say in the matter). A dilema that I did not know how to handle or feel about.

I wanted to make a friend without leaving the house I did not have any technology of any sort because it just did not appeal to me at all so I thought the best way to do this is through the ouija board and it would just be a conversation between me and my board no wires, no switching anything on, no typing, just a good old fashioned wooden board with words of the alphabet, a planchette and yes and no at both corners and the numbers 0 - 9 and goodbye underneath.

The Ouija board came into my life through my attic fell out of my bag which I put ready for the bin and onto my landing floor and from there ended up on my living room table where I have spent the last few weeks contemplating using it to make a friend not just any friend but a friend from many moons ago atleast that was my hope but I was still afraid to use it and would my Imagination and my fear take over me that something might happen to frighten me off using the board.

One night I decided to pull the Ouija board out of the bag and just lay it on my table with it's planchette laying on it there it was ready to be used but it was not fare to give the board such a hard time just because there was so much fear in my life and I already related the board with evil and satan before I even used it. Maybe a relative would come into my life and want to make contact with me but I just could not get evil out of my mind and my contact would be evil I just knew and had a sense that evil would come through to me in some shape or form. Some might say that if you think about evil and you deem the board as evil whilst using it then obviously evil will come through but one way or the other I just felt that this was not a good thing to do but what do human beings so often do go ahead and do it anyway.

The night was drawing on and I was sat there looking at the board and thought well it is now or never if nothing happens I will throw it away and forget the whole thing but I had a feeling something would happen because I always thought there is much more to life than just us humans and the here and now and there is so much history out there of a time on planet earth since the world began.

I sat by the table and put all the lights on inside my house my hands were shaking and my body sweating with fear my instincts were not to do this but my curiosity overwhelmed me as I was a human being after all. Out of the blue the curtain in my room waved in the air and went back down there were no windows open or any draft coming through the house as you can Imagine I went pale and cold and then I felt a breeze walk through me I sat in my chair frozen with fear not being able to move and then before I even touched the board the planchette moved on it's own by this point I ran out of the house and into my front yard it was pitch black but I was out of the house.

I kept my front door open and all the lights were on in the house and I just looked in through my windows I could not make out if I was being silly and using my Imagination for all of this or was there really supernatural forces going on around me because this board was ready to be used and was there an entity waiting in the room for me to make contact with a spirit or an evil entity through the board had I already gone to far by leaving the board open on my table like an ornament whatever it was it already knew I wanted to play.

I was afraid of being outside as I was inside because outside there could be a evil person ready to attack me and come into my house and Inside there could be an evil person waiting to attack me I could not win.

I did not know what to do be brave go back inside and throw the board out or see this through and make communication which is what I think the board wanted me to do but I had to think of my own safety and my own well being and could this do damage to my health or was I just being foolish. I so wanted to make communication with something or somebody I wanted to speak to somebody who had lived in a world that was so different to the one today and I was hoping we could compare notes and maybe I could make the world a better place through their advice.

I walked back into the house my body limp with fear and my legs trembling I closed the front door behind me and walked back into my living room and just stared at the ouija board out of the blue once again the chair by the table moved ready for me to sit down I stood there and cried my eyes out I could not move from the spot I was frozen with fear and I could feel my blood drain from my body, all of a sudden I felt a hand on my shoulder and it squeezed me by this time I could not feel my own body and my legs just stopped working fear had taken control of my bodily functions I unfortunetly wet myself and shit myself at the same time I had totally lost control of my bodily internal organs aswell as my outer limbs and functions.

The planchette moved and spelled out do not be afraid I am a friend. How could a friend put me through so much fear but this was not no ordinary friend this was somebody who had sensed my overwhelming desire to use the board and make contact even before I had touched the thing myself.

I could not be no more afraid than I already was the blood in my veins returned and as you can Imagine I was smelling of urine and faescous my legs returned to me I walked to my bathroom and took all of my clothes off I got into my shower and my body was still numb with fear my shower curtain was torn off the rail and my soap and shampoo and toothbrush thrown across the room I could hear the chair down stairs banging on the floor because it was ready for me to use the ouija board and for us to talk.

If I had wanted to I could have run out of the house into the pitch black and never returned or I could have picked up the board and ran with it and thrown it as far away as I could but this was what I wanted I wanted to make contact and it was ready for me to do this But was I ready for this and what forces was I dealing with here. I went downstairs and I walked over to the table and sat on the still chair that was wobbling all over the place just 2 mins ago the ouija board was ready for me to make contact as the planchette ran down the board ready for me to talk.

I could feel a prescence standing over me looking and watching what I was doing as if it was waiting to be released through the board or was it watching and keeping an eye on what I was doing I could not believe this was happening to me the one thing I feared in life was things beyond our comprehension things beyond human life on planet earth and a huge reason why I had not taken my own life many times was because I was afraid of what was next for us after death.

I could not have been more scared or petrified than I was it was either run from my room and run as far away as I could and never return and never talk about this to another human soul or go ahead with this and see where I go or see where we go.

I decided to make contact simply because I do not feel the prescence in the room would have let me go anyway and what if it wanted to kill me.

I put my hands on the planchette and asked the ouija board a question. 'I asked it are you going to hurt me?' the planchette went to 'no' (I could not belive this was happening) I then asked it could I make contact with an ancient homosexual possibly a Roman slave or a male roman prostitute the planchette moved again and spelt out why? 'I replied because maybe he could help me out with being gay and he could relate to the pain of it!' The planchette moved again and spelt out' What pain!'.

'Well I replied the pain of being gay even in his time and the pain of living to please others. The planchette moved again to' yes.' Had I made contact with an ancient slave boy or an ancient sex slave who lived in a time full of pain to live to please others or had the board tricked me and if so who on earth was I talking to.

I asked it one more question 'are you evil' ? the planchette ran between yes and no it was already playing games with me, I asked it again' I do not like playing games'?.

The planchette continued to run all over the board it was showing me who was boss and all of a sudden stopped on no!. I did not believe it was telling me the truth and I did not want to push my luck with it, but I pushed my luck and replied "are you telling me the truth"? the lamp in my room was thrown across the room and smashed on the wall it was letting me know not to push my luck and that the forces were a lot more powerful than I was. What had I got myself into.

I asked it did you live in the roman times ? the planchette went to 'yes.' It then went to the alphabet and spelt out 'they were cruel to me 'they used to hurt me and make me do things I did not want to do my body would hurt and bleed from the beatings and sexual cruelty put upon me'.

I responded by 'can I help you' the planchette went to 'yes' I said "how" it replied 'It is how I can help you we can help each other'.

I decided to go to bed as I had had enough of the day I was petrified to go to bed but I was mentally and physically exhausted and put a towel over the ouija board I went upstairs and got straight into bed I left my light on and as you can Imagine I was too scared to close my eyes I left my bedroom window open and the curtains open full I did not want to hear the silence of my room but I wanted to hear the owls and dogs barking from the house half a mile away any noise was better than the silence of the night in a very quiet old house.

My bedroom curtains were blowing in the wind and the cold air from the outside was blowing over me and under my sheets which I had shrouded my whole body in I felt a prescence in my room and it was not going to leave me alone until I had finished my conversation with whom ever I was in contact with through the ouija board.

I managed to get off to sleep I was fighting trying to go to sleep but the more you fight it the more you just fall into a sleep and off to sleep I went with my window wide open and the cold breeze and night air coming into my room along with anybody or anything entering my room if it wanted too. I was so scared that I was afraid of both anything in this world coming into my room and anything from another time already being in my room.

I had a dream as I was sleeping of a town with pebbled stones on the floor and people walking about in daylight there were market stalls and people walking around in old cloths for clothes carrying sacks on their backs and looking warn out. I was in some sort of a small town and the place looked old and warn and poor but the weather was hot and I was thirsty and my body was aching especially my back and my shoulders and my hands were bruised and bleeding and full of rough skin from some sort of scrubbing or hard manual work.. I was a young man as I could see from my body and my youth.

I kept on walking and I was trying to make contact with the people to ask them where I was and what was I doing here but nobody would look at me it was as if the whole town was scared to converse or even look at each other. Then some huge man in an Iron armour put sacks on my back which were heavy and I nearly fell to the ground trying to carry them. I could not carry them so the man In the Iron armour grabbed my arm and dragged me to a house where he took me straight to the kitchen of the house it was as if I had to remain in the kitchen as If the kitchen was my place to be, there was a person sat in the other room sitting by a table he was wearing black and his face was covered by a hood it was as if he was waiting for his food.

I saw food prepared on the kitchen table and a woman walked into the room she was an attractive woman and she had no clothes on she looked at me and gave me a smile and handed me the food to take to the person sitting by the table, I was tembling but she pointed to take the food to the other room. I took hold of the food and she took off my rags that I was wearing exposing my naked body the woman spoke and said "now slave boy now the master is hungry".

I took the food into the other room shaking and went to the person in the black clothing all of a sudden it got up off it's chair and took off it's hood and black robe it was an enormous man well built about 7 feet tall and full of muscles he looked like a huge warrior with a lot of command under him. He was totally naked too and ate the food I gave him I did not move off the spot and watched him eat. He then grabbed my arm and dragged me to his bedroom where he threw me onto the bed he was much much bigger than me he then physically pinned me face down on his bed where he forced himself on top of my back and penetrated me over and over and over.

I was screaming and screaming because it was so painful when the naked woman walked in she grabbed me picked me up in the air and threw me across the room where I woke up soaking wet and frozen with fear.

My bedroom was freezing cold and my curtains were hanging out the window there were leaves in my room and things had blown off the walls and off my shelves where the window had been open all night long the next thing my bed clothes were being quietly pulled off me the prescence in my room had been with me all night long. I got up my legs were shaking and my heart was pounding out of my chest and I was sick and tired of being scared all the time. I was used to being scared of real human beings but I was not used to being scared of an Invisible prescence watching my every move I knew it was there and I had to deal with it but I still did not know what it wanted from me. I closed my window and I had hoped that this had just been a bad dream but reality hit me that this was real and then all of a sudden I could hear banging downstairs I quietly crept downstairs and once again the chair was banging up and down and this time the table was too which had the ouija board on it the towel came off the table and was thrown across the room.

It wanted me to sit down and play again what choice did I have, I sat down and washed my hands over my face to wake myself up the next thing the planchette was racing across the board I asked the question 'please would you leave me alone the planchette went to' no 'I replied why I am scared' I put my hands on the planchette and it spelt out 'you asked for me to help you', I replied 'I have changed my mind please leave me alone' the planchette ran again to 'no 'it then spelt out I am a friend'. I replied but I am scared of you 'the planchette did not move for the first time, I replied again' are you the roman slave guy in my dreams 'the planchette went to yes.

I then felt that hand again on my shoulder I could feel my colour fade from my body and my blood run cold with fear, I replied I would like you to leave my house 'the planchette went to no no no no. I replied 'I do not need you anymore' the planchette spelt out 'you do', I replied why do I need you ', the planchette spelt out ' because you hate homosexual people ' I replied ' I do not hate homosexual people at all I am just afraid of them why would I hate homosexuals when we are both homosexuals.' The planchette spelt out why are you afraid ' I replied because they see straight through me we know each other and they become a threat to me '.

It replied "but I am in so much pain like you we need each other" (it was playing on my emotions and my Insecurities) I replied "I do not need you".

Look I said ' I do not hate homosexuals because I am a homosexual and I would never hurt anybody so please leave now and I am going to throw this board in the rubbish. ' It spelt out watch this ' all of a sudden all the doors closed in the house and all the curtains closed all the light bulbs smashed and all the furniture was being thrown across the room somebody then grabbed my neck and picked me up about 10 foot in the air I was being chocked and there was no way this was the slave guy in my dreams this was something else my clothes were being torn from my body and I was fighting pure air, I was pinned onto the table where the ouija board was and I was then turned over onto my stomach where I was penetrated up my bum by something enormous and very painful I screamed and screamed in pain just like in the dream and I thought my anus had been snapped in two.

I could not see anything as the room was pitch black I was then turned over onto my back and knocked out by what seemed like a hammer for a fist.

I woke up my face aching and bleeding and my bum hurting and feeling very very sore the room was a mess in fact turned upside down and I managed to get up and get hold of the ouija board which was on the floor also I put it on the table with the planchette and asked it why did you do this ' it replied I am now inside you and I am going to help you. I was now possesed by something and I did not know what it was or what it wanted from me. It was in control of my body and there would be nothing I could do about it.

It cleaned the house and put all the furniture back the thing inside my body acted like a proper human being it knew what I got up to in the days and nights and functioned just like I would it was very clever and knew exactly how to decieve people and act normal.

I would go to bed at night and have the same dreams over and over walking into a room a very dark room the curtains blowing in the air but there was no air but the curtains were blowing and I walked closer to the window and I could see no glass in the window just empty blackness

I try to walk away from the window because I am afraid as to what is behind the darkness when I wake up in a cold sweat and shaking.

As I am asleep I can feel myself being trapped in a body that is not my own it is only when I am asleep that I feel free it's as if it is not at it's strongest when my body is asleep but it is so scary because I am lying in a dark room my body asleep but it is not really me.

I still do not know what this thing wants with my body and I still do not understand why it was so brutal towards me during the possesion I was so afraid of evil entering my life and I had helped it all along to enter my life.

I went to work I ate food I bathed I did everything I always did but there was a difference to me and I was now getting the picture as to what it wanted my body for and as I suspected it would not be for good reasons. Whatever was Inside me I knew it had had a bad life in it's time and of course I was going through a rough time we fed off each other but there was a huge distinction between us because I would never hurt anybody but it was not up to me what my body or my actions did when around other gay men.

It was a friday night and I found myself doing something I would never normally do and I knew this was where the trouble would start and I was absolutely powerless to stop it.

I got into the shower and then as I was cleaning my teeth looked into the mirror and could see a person it was me but it was a shell of me I did not know who the person in the mirror was or even what he wanted with my body. I went into the bedroom and put on my best clothes which I would normally wear to work functions and I found myself going out and walking amongst night clubs gay nightclubs places I would never normally go to for obvious reasons and places which scared me to death.

I walked in and there were men everywhere dancing and talking in the corridors and kissing and looking at me I must have been new meat to them and somebody they were going to argue over.

It was as if this thing inside my body was playing on my fears and Insecurities and it was taking my body to places which frightened me to death it was like it was using my body to get to me and to get to other people I can only describe this as pure evil.

There were gay eyes everywhere or gaydar and fuck me stares left right and centre and my body was flirting with all the men and dancing with them and kissing them it was as if a repressed body and mind was all of a sudden going out of control and wanting to fuck anybody in sight the possession was using my inner convictions and fears to go wild and display my sexuality for all to see from a repressed homosexual to a screaming loud and proud queen and I hated every second of it but I had no control to stop it.

There was a guy who came up to me he was very handsome and young maybe a student or young executive he was smart and looked like he was loaded with money his eyes were piercing blue and he had lovely blond hair a proper hunky handsome guy who could have anybody he wanted but he picked me why I do not know as I am of plain looks and not a guy you would deem as handsome or cute.

I feel it was a trance I feel the thing inside me hypnotised him to fall for me and he was hooked my body asked him "do you want to come back to my place" I wanted to scream and break out of my body and say no I do not want you to come back to my place I am not like that how dare you abuse my body like this I have never even been Intimate with anybody you are stealing my virginity. My body had already been raped by evil forces but now it was letting a human being seed me aswell it was torturing me but It thinks it is helping me but how?. my virginity was very Important to me and I was waiting for somebody special to take it but I had waited for nothing evil had stolen my Innocence. I had no chance the guy and my body were hooked with each other and my virginity was to be taken and there was nothing I could do about it I was screaming inside but nobody could hear me.

Back to the house we went and the guy could not believe how Isolated my house was we were both very drunk and he was looking around the house and came across the ouija board "oh a fucking ouija board he said I have got to play this" when he sat down to play it it went straight to goodbye and jumped off the table and on the floor, my body ran into the room and grabbed him and said "stay away from it, do you understand me you never touch that", he said "chill man chill how did that fucking thing jump off the fucking table weird man really weird", my body then grabbed him and took him into the bedroom my body ripped his clothes off him and pinned him to the bed, "hey man he said calm it down not so fucking rough" I was powerless to stop this happening and all I could do is watch as my body was hurting other people something I never ever wanted it to do because I would never do it.

The guy was pinned to the bed and now he was having sex with something that was inside me the guy said "I have condoms I always use condoms," my body replied we are not using those as I must let loose inside you, "the guy told my body to fuck off and let him go as he felt uncomfortable" my body slapped the guy across the face and kept punching him all over his body my body lay on top of the guy and with supreme force my body put the guy on his front and inserted my penis inside his anus where my penis cummed inside him, the guy cried and screamed he had sex without his consent to it and so had I we had both been victims of rape but raped by a thing we had no knowledge of or why it was doing this but one thing I did know I had released something to take possession of me and I was stuck in a body that was not my own the guy curled up into a ball on the bed and then the same thing that had happened to me after I was raped my body punched the guy in the face and knocked him out cold this thing inside me was very powerful both physically and pyschologically.

The next day the guy got up from bed and was sore and swolen and he burst out crying I was lying next to him he had slept through the night from pure exhaustion and brutality on the body he said "I thought you were ok you seemed ok I will go straight to the police" my body grabbed his jaw and said "(In a most evil and gruesome voice) If you go to the police or you mention the trauma you have been through here or even mention my name or where I live I will find your family and slaughter them all." The guy went pale and his lips blood red his hair standing on end and his eyes red and bloodshot just walked out of the house quietly in disbelief of what he had seen and more to the point what had he been raped by and what evil seed did he have inside him.

Evil is very smart and it had to show itself in it's true form to protect itself from the law. It knew that it had to scare it's victims in the best way possible so they would not talk to anybody about this ordeal and even if they did who would believe them.

Two days went by and my body spent most of the time lying in bed and staring at the ceiling I was a prisoner in my own body in my own house and I was powerless to do anything about it I put the tv on in the bedroom when the news came on it was a picture of the guy who came to my house and had sex with my body or with the thing that possessed my body he had died of unatural and mysterious causes that doctors could not explain. The thing inside my body burst out laughing and shouted out I fucking got him "now I really knew what this thing inside me wanted it wanted to seed gay guys with it's cum poision it was using my fear's and it's evilness to kill other gay men in the modern world and I helped let this happen. My body spoke to me and said" this could turn out to be an epedemic to hundreds of gay men". It was going to kill many many more and it was using my body to do it and I was absolutely powerless to stop it.

I would go and visit family and act natural and there was no way in the world I was going to let it hurt my family I would eat normally and talk normally and I made sure there was no paranormal activity at my family home. I needed this to stop and I needed to get this thing out of my body but I could not think of a way to do this and I was all alone.

I had the dream again that night I was in the same town and the same village and I was watching the slave guy getting beaten by his master he was naked and pinned up against the wall and whipped over and over and he was made to go and get wine with his back bleeding and sore and him barely even able to walk. When he came back with the wine the master drank it and pinned him to the bed and raped him over and over. I was looking at him in sobs and sobs of tears and I was powerless to help him when the slave guy saw me and looked at me and said "please help me please release me" the master looked at me too and laughed and then out of no where spat in my face and laughed you are both powerless to kill me I will torture you both.

Then the naked woman came into the room as she always did and picked me up and threw me across the room where I woke up and thought the master has possessed me and he is keeping me and the slave guy prisoner evil is well and truly with me and it was free out in the world through me.

My body was stuck with an ancient homosexual or bisexual roman master inside it and it was destructive to hurt and kill other gay men it was tormenting and playing with me psychologically and it was hurting it's slave and making me watch through my dreams. I was in hell through my own world and through another time there was nobody I could turn to for help and I knew I had break away from the evil Inside me but I was helpless to breaking free and I did not have a clue where to even start.

There was a thought I had and that was too make contact with the slave guy through my dreams and maybe asking him for help or asking him if he knew of a way to break this evil and kill his master but how would I do this without the possession knowing about it because he knew everything I was thinking and my every move.

But I had to try it what more could it do to punish me it already had possession of my body and it was haunting both my body and my mind maybe it was trying to kill me to kill my soul so then it would have total control and be back in the modern world to release evil upon humanity. I could never allow this to happen there was one way I could kill the thing but my thoughts were I would also die in the process. I would have to sacrifice myself to kill the evil it seemed the only way out.

Once again friday came and once again I found myself getting ready to go out on the town and I thought oh no another victim is going to die and I was screaming inside no no no please don't hurt anybody more, all I could hear was laughter and for the first time a voice and the voice said ' this is what you wanted '.

It was playing with my mind once again maybe I did want to hurt other homosexuals but it was just a thought and I only thought this because I was jelous of them and envious of them but I would never ever carry out that thought never it truly was using my negative and disturbing thoughts that were Intrusive to my mind to kill others and maybe I asked for this to happen through my mind and that was what it was feeding off.

It was now making me feel guilty and withdrawn and the evil was working to maybe kill me and take over my body altogether I had to be strong and I had to fight back somehow.

Out on the town my body went and yes once again I came home with another victim I wanted to scream out to him ' you are going to die ' but it was not me and he would not hear me trapped in my own body. Into the bedroom we went and exactly the same as before the guy was beaten and tortured and seeded by the master I had no choice once again but to watch my own body inflict cruelty and suffering on another human being.

The guy got up and left the following day with bruises over his face and body he walked away screaming ' you bastard you evil bastard ' the master responded by saying exactly the same he had said to the first victim ' the guy responded by saying "What are you and why me" the guy walked away and said ' your a psycho your a fucking psycho ' and he ran from the house.

Then once again on the news came the guy's face and the news reader said "another man dies of a mystery Illness that is baffling medics and it has been confirmed that both men were homosexual.". I was crying inside while the master was laughing on the outside.

I could not allow the master to hurt anybody else in his time or my own time but how could I stop him and would I ever be able to stop him maybe I was trapped in hell forever and I was still alive in the process.

It suddenly occured to me that it had used the slave guy to contact me as the master did not want to make contact with me himself maybe he was not allowed to make contact from the dead or maybe he was afraid to make contact but he had used the slave guy to trick me to talk to it and feel pity for it the master was watching me all along playing with the board and it had already entered my house even before it took over my body I just helped it make it's way back into the world from the dead or was it a much much bigger force than the master?.

Out of the blue one day there was a knock at my door I never had any visitors to the house so as you can Imagine I wondered who this was I went to the door and there was a man there with a suit on and a long black coat he said "I am a detective Inspector with the police he then said can I come in and talk" I said "well yes of course what is this about" "well he said we have been watching some cctv footage from the nightclubs you visited over the past 2 weeks and we saw you leave the clubs with the two deceased men in the news lately and he mentioned their names" I asked the policeman "Can I ask sir how did you get my address," the policeman responded

"I am a detective sir it's my Job" "Oh right I said yes isn't it awfull" I was hoping that this police man could help me and he would see that there was a total monster here that he was talking too and I was hoping that the master would slip up and that he would be arrested.

I said to the police man "what do you want to ask me" "well lets look here, you were seen with these men you were seen leaving with these men and then they end up dead" "well for your Information yes I am gay and I enjoy lots of sex yes these men came back here we had sex they left the following day and that's that it's very sad that they are both now dead but that's how I knew them".

"The detective asked" and are you ok with your health no problems" "well I hope not" "the police man asked you know both the men did not speak to their families and the reason was because they were gay" "No I said, I did not know this about them as I said I just brought them back here and we had sex and well there was no real conversation at all". "well said the police man I suggest you go and get yourself checked out with your doctor and I will be in touch if anything else comes to light" "ok I said bye bye then" I was mad that the master used his charm on the police man and I was mad that the master had killed guys who had come through so much personal problems in their lives and were looking to get on with their lives he had prayed on the vunerable once again.

I would have to try and contact the slave guy somehow in my next dream and ask him if he knew how to kill his master and maybe me and the slave guy could do it together and find peace with ourselves. I could not allow any more guys to die.

It was not long before the dream came again and the same thing happened as it does in all the dreams and I was watching everything I watched the master being waited on by the slave then the naked woman walked into the room and told the slave to please the master with his body after watching the slave go through sexual torture with the master and the naked woman I hid away hoping the naked woman would not see me and throw me across the room.

The master went to sleep as my body spent most of it's time when not in work asleep and just lying in bed and the slave guy had to go and wash the dishes and clean the kitchen while the naked woman watched over her master like a gaurd dog.

I managed to creep to the kitchen and talk to the slave he was crying and hurting and washing the dishes and I said "hey slave" he looked at me and said "souls are not allowed in here souls do not speak to us how did you escape" "I said what do you mean escape" "If the naked lady finds you she will lock your soul away in the kingdom of lost souls" "I said what is the kingdom of lost souls" "it is a place that means you will have to spend time trapped in a place you originally came from and haunt and hurt people" "so the master is a lost soul" "yes he said he is trapped in your body and I am trapped here by the naked lady".

"so who is the naked lady" the slave guy replied "she is evil upon evil a most dangerous demon she keeps people prisoner she is in charge of all the demons she may look beautiful but she is a horrid evil entity." "I asked do you know satan" he went pale and looked away we never ever talk about him not even the naked lady talks about him", "I asked how do I kill the master to release my soul" the slave replied I think you already know "I was trapped in the bowels of hell.

All of a sudden the naked lady ran into the kitchen and picked me up and threw me across the room I screamed out ' fuck off me leave me ' she then licked my face with a tongue that I had only seen on a snake she wispered in my ear "you will be mine very soon".

I woke up and I felt the naked woman getting closer to me I could not allow her to take my soul or to kill any other people or even worse let her take over my body so she can walk on planet earth once again. I had to stop her but I felt the only way to do this was to kill myself to break free.

I would have to find a way of killing myself and freeing my soul without the naked woman finding out my thoughts and stopping me altogether and taking over my body altogether and my soul. I did not want to die as I had wanted to die so very much growing up because I was not a happy person growing up but suicide was something I could never go through with but now all of this had happened I could not allow my body to keep killing people and I did not want to be a prisoner in my own body anymore.

I would need the slave's help to do this because the naked lady controlled both the slave and the master and me too through them so I came up with the plan that if the slave finds a way of locking up the naked lady I would be able to dispose of the ouija board and then I would climb up on top of the roof of my house and jump off I was not scared because this was not me killing myself this was me killing an ancient demon who was very close to totally possessing my body.

The naked lady had far too much power through the master to let me do this but if my plan worked and I was able get rid of her at just the right time then my mission would be done and I would have saved myself and humanity too.

In my next dream I was able to make contact with the slave guy and tell him my plan I told him that when the slave rapes you after his food and the naked lady is alone with the master while he sleeps you must call the naked lady into the kitchen and keep her busy while I get rid of the ouija board and throw myself off the roof of the house. I told him this can only be done while she is out of the room and the master is asleep that is when he is at his weakest.

The slave guy told me he will do this on one condition that I come back for him and take him with me it was a chance I would have to take letting my soul go back to the house of the master and the naked lady to save the slave it could mean the naked lady trapping my soul forever like she had to so many other souls but she would never be able to enter my body and possess my body or any other body through the board in my house but if evil wins over good she just might be able to have my soul for ever and ever and I would once again be trapped.

This was all a conflict of good vs evil but I had to be strong and I had to make this work or her power would be massive in my world of today and I had to stop her once and for all, evil prays on the weak but one thing I had over the naked lady was that I was willing to give my own life to kill her and that was a huge sacrifice in itself.

I now had it all planned it was a thursday night and I had to do this tonight before another friday night came and there would be another victim the police had no evidence at all to convict me of the crimes they were just lost with this case as far as they were concerened the victims came to my house and they left my house and then died of natural causes this could happen over and over and over until hundreds upon hundreds of gay men were dead and there would be nothing to stop the evil inside me from doing this.

There was something inside me that had poision for sperm or whatever it was that killed gay men a little while after they had had sex with me but it made out it was due to natural causes it was as if it ate up the insides of a human gay male.

It would baffle the police, doctors, scientists, and people and it certainly made gay men very very wary of who they Interacted with and that sex was not top of their priority on a first date or a first glance and it petrified the gay community in the area.

I had to wait for the dream to happen again and it had to be exact for this to work I would have to be in contact with the ancient world and the people there that were heavily involved in taking over my body for good. The dream came and it was time for hopefully good to triumph over evil the same thing happened as usual this was good because then nothing was different or unusual I was watching while the salve was taking the food into the master the naked lady was watching the slave take the food into him, once the master finished his food he grabbed the slave as normal and raped him this was always painfull for me to watch everytime then the naked lady would walk into the room while the slave went into the kitchen to do the washing up then the master would lie on his bed while the naked lady lay with him protecting him and waiting just waiting for the full possession of me to happen when this would occur I do not know but I could never allow this to happen she was waiting very very patiently for my soul.

As planned I hid well away not for the naked lady to see me and the slave boy called out "come come come" the naked lady ran from her bed with the master to see what disobidience the slave was calling out next I heard the slave close the door behind her and grab the kitchen table to block against it. I heard he scream out "how dare you I will burn your soul forever in flames for this", I managed to wake up through fear as we so often do if our dreams become too much for us bear and I ran to the ouija board and set fire to it it went up in flames as so did the table and most of the house I then climed the ladder I had put there ready to climb to the roof of my house which I did and got to the top without hesitation and with my house burning down

I jumped and from there I was in a place which I can only describe as pure hell itself.

I was in a very dark place full of the most ugly and grotesque creatures with a smell that I cannot even describe there were screams which seemed like people being tortured and crying coming from everywhere there seemed to be conflicts going on between people fighting their pain while being tortured and the things torturing them taking delight and sexual gratification in doing this they seemed to get pleasure from this and there were lots of humongous and giant penis's everywhere a place to me which seemed like sexual torture and gratification but a place no sadio masicist or sexual perverse person would dare to want to go.

A creature came to me from out of the dark it was wearing a red robe or coat which was made of thick carpet like material and on the sleeves was red silk this person or what ever it was was very very important down here in this place the robe covered it's whole body apart from it's hands which were like the hands of an eagle skiny with huge giant razor sharp claws which could cut through skin like a knife.

It spoke to me with a voice that was deep and loud but very calm at the same time it said "you contacted me because you wanted help and then you decide to kill me, I am a very private person you know and I very very rarely communicate with your world". "But I said" are you the naked lady" "the naked lady works for me and she was working for me to take over your body I introduced you to three of my souls the slave, the master, and the naked lady, through these souls you wanted help from me to help you with your fear of your homosexuality" I said "you were killing other homosexuals this was not what I wanted at all" the voice suddenly became more angered "no but it is what I wanted I wanted their souls and you helped me get these through your own pathetic stupid human Insecurities" I said "well you will never achieve that now" it replied "oh really and you think some other idiot from the human race is not going try to contact me in future through one of my many boards.

It said "look where you are, look where you have ended up and you think you have escaped me you have just come into a place of eternal torture on your soul and you are mine not in body but in spirit and my time will come through some other lost soul there are many out there".

I asked "where is the slave is he safe, is he ok, from behind the cloak of the creature the salve apperared he grabbed me and clung onto me" the slave said "take me with you" the creature said "you are both mine and I will put you both in situations of pain and cruelty that you never thought possible" "I said I know who you are you are the creature we fear on planet earth and you weep your way into our humanity little by little" "oh yes it said I am always with you on planet earth I pray on the vunerable and the weak and people like you I feed off your Insecurities and you let me in" "Yes Lucifer I said I did let you in" (I had come face to face with the devil himself) he had come to take me in person I was not going to go without a fight I had already stopped the possession on my body in the real world and I was ready to fight for my soul I knew I just knew I did not belong here. I was a very powerful fighter pyscholigically and for the devil himself to come and get me I must have been a challenge and wasn't this going to be a fight. I had already beaten the master and the naked lady and I was going to fight not just for my soul but for the soul of the slave guy too.

"It said you do not speak my name", "so I said this is it your home" (I could understand the sexual torture because a huge part of the human race is sex and sex is what makes us come into the world and this is how the world keeps going without sex the human race and reproduction would die out, gay men could not reproduce and maybe this is what lucifer feared a world without reproduction through my contact with the board he was able to grow in me from my own insecurites about not leading a life of reproduction with a woman).

"I said I do not belong here I am a good person and so is the slave you made me into a monster and you want to keep me here through my own guilt about contacting you" "enough of this I will take you both to where you belong in the bowels of my home itself," it reached out and grabbed the salve by his hair while I was in the middle of them grabbing hold of the slave not letting evil have him or me when more creatures came from out of the dark pulling us towards lucifer and we were being swept further and further into darkness and into a cave there were screams and cries coming from everywhere and grotesque laughter my skin was bleeding from razor sharp claws that were grabbing me and cutting me like razor blades but I was still holding on to the slave determined not to let him go as I promised him he would be safe. "Hold on I said to the slave, don't let go I screamed out god help us please help us please help us poor souls",.

I heard one of the creatures say "him he is calling him I heared a cry saying get them here with us good must never have them a wind was blowing like a gale there were screams and demonic noises my skin was being torn apart by claws I still grabbed hold of the slave protecting him while others were trying to prize him away from me, I screamed again" please god please save us we are good my screams were piercing for dear life, Lucifer was shouting "no I will not lose them no I felt his claw on my back pushing me and the salve towards him, I screamed louder and I did not stop" god please please save us god god god you must come please we do not want to be here we do not belong here".

A light appeared out of the darkness a white light it was a large man with wings dressed in white and around him were lots of little other people dressed in white all with wings, Lucifer screamed out "how dare you come into my home these are mine their souls are mine" the larger man dressed in white did not speak but raised his hand to lucifer and with his finger just waved it back and four as if to say no these two are mine, the smaller people dressed in white came down for us and picked us both up the slave said to me "is this your god is this who you were screaming for" "yes I said this is him this is the person I promised I would take you too" we were both ripped to shreads and hardly alive as we were being flown away the grotesque demons were still trying to get us but the little people who were holding us were doing the same as the large man in white waving their finger to them as if to say no not these two they are in the wrong place.

Lucifer shouted out "there will always be some other poor soul who needs help" and I shouted back "and good will always be there to conquer if we ask for it in our lives". The devil just stared at me just a long dark evil stare as if to say this is not over by any means, but a stare that meant maybe I cannot help the next person and maybe the next person will not be as strong willed as I was to get good back into my life.

Me and the slave went a place of peace and comfort where there was an overwhelming sense of feeling good about yourself and our bodies felt fresh and good there was no fear anymore for me back on planet earth or for the slave in his world we were both two lost souls who could have been living a life of torture in the other world but I knew good would conquer evil I knew it in my heart that if I asked for help and I asked for the good path it would come and conquer the demons.

I knew I was a good person and I knew I did not belong in the demonic world and my Instincts did not let me down and I knew that the slave would be allowed to go with me as I knew there was good in his heart otherwise I would have never clung onto him as I did.

Me and the slave were always together in god's kingdom and we were always on the look out for lost souls who one day may need our help to escape the devil's claws just like we did we knew that if good saved us then one day we would return the favour to somebody who had unfortunetly gone to the wrong place but they so so much needed help to get to the right place.

The End.

Epilogue

After the fire and the house had burned down and my body had been found burnt to a crisp my family and work colleagues and the neighbours around the area just thought I had gone Insane and commited suicide by burning down my house and Jumping into the flames.

The police however thought it very strange that they questioned me over the deaths of two homosexual men and that I then go on to kill myself and then the strange deaths in the gay community suddenly stop.

The local papers had the headlines strange loner gets seen with the two deceased men and questioned by police then kills himself suddenly the deaths come to a stop. My family and work colleagues had no Idea I had anything to do with these men or about my habits and visits to the local gay scene. I guess they must have felt shocked and deceived by what they read but there again who did really know me.

I was unable to protect myself from all the media and everything that was said about me because I was just a lonely guy that happened to let evil into my life and let it pray on me through my vulnerabilities and who would believe my story even if I survived the fire all they would have done was lock me away in a mental Institution.

My reputation had been shattered and my family would have to suffer for this but I killed myself to save the world from the devil himself entering our universe and spreading it's evil spawn to kill others.

I was given my place in the kingdom of heaven for fighting the devil himself and having my soul released along with the slave for finding goodness in my heart and believing that good can always triumph over evil.

I was now in god's kingdom ready to do good work and save souls who lost their way but were asking for help to find their way into god's kingdom.

Evil will always pray on the scared and vunerable on planet earth and it will find some way to manifest itself onto humans but as I found out if your heart is good and you fight evil and it's demons then your soul will be rewarded by the almighty himself.

www.ingramcontent.com/pod-product-compliance
Lightning Source LLC
Chambersburg PA
CBHW020348110726
47898CB00003B/1096